DICHTEN =
No. THREE

Ilma Rakusa

S T E P P E

translated from the German
by Solveig Emerson

BURNING DECK, PROVIDENCE

1997

DICHTEN = is an annual of current writing in German (in English translation), edited by Rosmarie Waldrop. Most issues will be given to the work of a single author.

Individual copies: $10.
Subscription for 2 issues: $16.
In England: £5.
Subscription for 2 issues: £8. Postage 25p/copy.

Distributors:

Small Press Distribution, 1341 Seventh St., Berkeley, CA 94710
Spectacular Diseases, c/o Paul Green, 83b London Rd., Peterborough, Cambs. PE2 9BS

for US subscriptions only:
Burning Deck, 71 Elmgrove Ave., Providence RI 02906

This volume is made possible by a grant from the Schweizer Kulturstiftung Pro Helvetia.
Burning Deck is the literature program of Anyart: Contemporary Arts Center, a tax-exempt non-profit corporation.

ISSN 1077-4203
ISBN 1-886224-27-7

Cover by Keith Waldrop

CONTENTS

Half-time

1

WHAT IS IT they say: the die is cast. A wanted to, with B. B wanted to, with A. Nothing to be done. Something didn't want A with B and B with A. Something might be a puppy. Just look at that puddle on the parquet. Then the spitz would have run across the stage and diverted the couple. Would have made his mark. Anna Fyodorovna, allow me. And you, Maestro, be off and report. The cheeky imp that clears the air. The curtain raised before an ever empty set.

2

WHILE THE SNOW covering the path, the mountain road, the main road, the ring road piles higher and higher, and the drivers' fears grow, I ask myself what there is to regret. Birdsong. No, nothing at all. After ten years of provincial life I ask things out of pure ignorance, things which I shouldn't ask. How are things with your brother Herman? Answer: mentally ill. He's the lost hope of the family. And didn't those two want a divorce? The snow deadens the noise, I regret nothing at all. After ten years of provincial life, I ask myself whether I'm in the dreamt-of future. The past is dust, and your boy, has he done his Finals? That's how to draw out a get-together in a café. The person you asked shakes his head, the boy works in a tree nursery. Wonderful, wonderful. Certainly, I say, one must move forwards, make discoveries with shears and. I love tumult. The widower looks me over thoroughly. The tree nursery is snowed in, but what makes me into an intruder? After ten years of provincial life, I practise being lonely in well-cut clothes. I regret nothing at all. When the conversation becomes repetitive the gardener enters. Herman is conquering a new world for himself. The widower swears: marriage is a *tête à tête*. I have freed myself from my masters.

3

THE FOREST, the path through the forest and the puppy, lively. Spitz is silent out of politeness, whilst They disturb. Talk themselves into believing the forest is a surgery. Child and school attendance and exams. A quotes herself, B quotes A, A quotes B, therefore herself. The sky is alone. Spitz develops a hatred of the couple, who cruelly assert rights. If they get close to the subject, the big questions, then everything rhymes like shut your mouth with good morning. A hopes B's sleep is destroyed, B makes his jealousy so important that the forest floor shakes. Spitz' fur shimmers like white skirt-lining. Spitz wanders aimlessly through the demoniac nature of the quarrellers until he hears silence.

4

I THINK I'M MIXING something up. I think the flurry of snowflakes dates from back when the snow was my professional secret. I wandered aimlessly through Russian snowstorms. The search was ended by a shot. I forget, I remember. There was a bridegroom, a bride. They missed each other. After a one-hour wait he gave out a cry of distress: I implore you by your red calico shirt, I implore you by your lips, I implore you by Saint Paraskeva: come. Fate, or what is it they say. Giggled unappetisingly. There was no reply. She travelled in the sled, in the opposite direction, freed from every stirring of will. The fur across her lap. A jagged knife in the fur. The wind had obliterated all borders. I don't know where forgetting begins. Snow deadens, that much is certain. I went back home, I washed my face, I leafed through my address book. I leafed through time. Others have approached Fate courageously. What does approach mean anyway.

5

BANG-BANG, SPITZ, get lost. The couple are so offensive that they succumb to every temptation to hate. Flexible, he says. I know that too, she says. Deep down I just know it. Why the pride in your heart? Snorting, he orders: silence. She sits at the desk with her arms hanging down. A gnome, she says to herself, that's what I am. That's what he's turned me into. Spitz! Has disappeared into the garden. Must she have a witness to her unhappiness? He doesn't use a shaving mirror, he interprets himself. Over her scraps of paper she thinks she wishes him an honest, frank nature. To monopolise unhappiness would be too cheap. Everywhere bits of alphabet that make you cry. With a slap on the shoulder she'll wish him a happy future. Him, the enlightened actor, B.

9

I ASK MYSELF what it means that I was born at such and such a
time in such and such a place, that after the sleet the thaw set in.
It's thawing. The chaffinches and great-tits etc. They're bathing
in the puddles. The brightness increases. Through the slit in the
lamp medical light seeps out. The moon in the house, where was
it when. Crescent-shaped over the factory building. I first saw
the light of the world. I cried myself alive. I haven't cried since.
After ten years of provincial life, the cries of the city are
deafening. I wear the colour of grass. Someone says: placid, he
hardly knows me. In my hand two marriages are foreseen. Two
short cuts (lines). Neither will you ever cross the Atlantic. Alright
or not alright. That still leaves hopes for the Taklamahan desert.
Feeling my way from grass blade to grass blade along its jagged
edge, resting on three grains of salt. After ten years of provincial
life, No-Man's-Land appeals to me. A Nobody. The Gobi-
Express.

B: I'll do the opposite.
A: Of what?
B: I mean on principle.
A: I see.

Spitz strays more and more often into the neighbour's garden. In
his quest for tenderness he makes the whole area unsafe. He
barks, he overpowers box hedges, he chews up a child's ball.
Funny. The couple don't miss him. She kneels before a votive
picture, he smokes. United efforts, she cries. He has cleared off.
In the night Spitz meets his master, who is making his way home
with his collar turned up. The man needs extra help. And as for
her, she should take drastic measures, thinks Spitz.

A: That's what it's about.
B: But I don't understand it.
A: Blinkers drop from my eyes.
B: Adieu Adieu Adieu.

8

TWO TIMES TWO is five, before breakfast one iron tablet, unchewed, no I'm not in a bad mood. After ten years of provincial life everything happens in the present tense. I buy myself a watch, the watch is watertight, I write a circular letter, that serves me as cheerfulness. Everything is useable. There, the siskin is bathing too. Rosa is mad about free-time boyfriends and classless geckoes. I'm glad of our non-connection. After ten years of provincial life it's not even half-time. So I can confidently consider myself a nomad.

9

HERE AND THERE Spitz gets half a bone, or they risk the greeting: heel! B hardly ever shows himself, A has degenerated into such a misanthropist that she has to keep company with the animal. She says she's unreasonable. Spitz doesn't stop her. With a bright face, he protects her. Sleep overcomes her in broad daylight. A wild, ruffled sleep out of which she awakes with a sudden start. Where is B? In the sauna, in the library? Spitz keeps guard. Spitz is lying on the wine-red carpet with the nomadic design, head turned towards the door. Sweet, she says crying. They eat their evening meal together. In front of the box, she knows: she dreamt about a detective and a raven. An inseparable couple. Heel! Oh, there you are. Spitz isn't surprised anymore. And the safety lock snaps shut.

I REALLY AM. I really am happy. How? Well. After ten years of provincial life I'm taking heart. A municipal swimming pool! A floating theatre! No more missed chances. The road to the tree nursery leads straight back again. Into the smog-landscape, but what does it matter. Inverted atmosphere is what I like best. After ten years of provincial life there's nothing I wouldn't like best. The widower fears a decline. You too, he says, like Herman. You what? I say. He stammers: guideline, the absence of. My morning cocoa gives me great pleasure. Something is past, cast off *en bloc*. Kow-towing. From day to day the bird song grows stronger. From day to day I wake up. Stronger! My Zürich joy, the only one of its kind, follows the soprano line.

Vladimir

IT DOESN'T HAVE to be like that, he said. It could be different. What? I said. He stood apart from the stream of visitors, at peace with himself. The Futurism of the moment. Or is it that you love display cases? Insolent, he asked about my destiny. One or two things need a little more work, I said with a glance at the retrospective exhibition. Nothing against private publications, I particularly like to be involved with Russian pamphlets. Nevertheless. He was pleased. Kruchonykh 1914, Malevich 1916, Roaring Parnassus and whatever their names are, undamaged, under glass. You love? Oh, I said, in a historical sense, yes.

We stood by the canal. There were two colours in the water and a current which allowed no conclusions. Unsingle-minded, I added. I love what I don't know. He buried his hands in his jacket pockets. The usual, he said. Woman won't show her true colours. You look distraught.

Me? He looked for my reflection. The futuristic stopgaps are leading you into a retrograde dependence, rent a palace.

Palace, I said. Judge for yourself.

He ran his hand over my worn-out jeans. A straw hat, and you'd be the loveliest cloud in trousers.

Please, I said. Please don't trap me in the narrow limits of your imagination. If there were an anti-canal, then.

He objected to the conditional. He named the colours of the canal: grey, green. You can't have anything against that. You could choose the crowd too.

As I pulled his hand out of his jacket pocket several palace reforms went through my mind. I didn't associate anything else with palaces.

Well? he asked.

How about a coffee, I said.

In the bar there were five mirrors and a shining assortment of bottles. We leaned against the counter. Futuristic motion-hysteria, he said, speed-madness.

Look at this Cinzano advertisement.

Writing, I said. Brought to a standstill.

He looked me over with a sideways glance, as you might a bird, an insect, a whore.

Purple, I said. Unsuspicious.

He slurped the foam from his coffee. Exactly, the silence between the characters.

All at once I knew what he meant. Master, I said timidly, of the spaces.

Let's stick to Cinzano. You take it with ice, I take it without.

He laid his hand on my shoulder. The rest you've got right.

Perhaps a Grappa would be better, I said.

You?

Never lewd, he said of himself, immune to futuristic temptations as opposed to...

I know, I said. I know your type.

I wanted to tell him to go to hell. In case you deny me the future, I'm making a pact with it!

He took on the look of a prisoner and quoted Mayakovsky, 1930.

What's that for, I said.

The future cost him his life.

You mean love.

I dragged him out of the bar. We ran through alleys and over bridges, I allowed him no standstill. To the ghetto, he called, or I'll end this sentimental journey in a canal. So that's how to show your true colours, I mocked. I was far ahead of him. As though my life were at stake, I hurried in the direction given, away from the streams of visitors.

We stopped in a square, panting. Tree-less, unfuturistically solitary. Nothing about the scenery disturbed me, only his dandy's jacket. We sat down on a bench. I drummed a tune on the wood, he was lost in his thoughts, God knows where. I drummed on. That's right, he said. I saw sounds into sentences till early morning like a half-crazed jeweller. What's right? I interrupted him. The rhythm, he said. Even of this square that originally wasn't a square. What was it then? Synagogue with courtyard, if that's enough. He had historical details at his fingertips, but that wasn't what it was about. I sought him on the other side of quotation. In the same place he wanted me.

We won't get far in one round.

How far do you want to get then?

Here were three sparse, newly planted beds in the square, which could honestly be called tree-less: up to that willow branch and back.

Because the squalor of this area is so moving?

I walked two steps behind him, the checked pattern on his jacket started to flicker, I raised my head and saw, above me, an arm shaking out a black duster. Like a new beginning, I scanned, using Arabic ordinals. We weren't running a race. Firstly, I thought, the barrenness of this place leaves only hope. Secondly, I know all about how to wait. Thirdly, everybody needs someone with a clear head. Now we were walking alongside each other. Think, he said, about who lost face in 1930, Mayakovsky or the hosts of literary bureaucrats. Mon Dieu, I said. Precious kitty, doesn't that sound nice?

15

I took his arm, one couldn't be more intimate. The bureaucrats, I said. Something connects them with the crowds.

In the ghetto square he described how Mayakovsky fled with long strides (jibes) from un-love, while the »human jungle began to haggle«. The puppy in him had been Lilya's creature. A melancholy whinge. Even the puppy had run away.

Are you called Vladimir?

What makes you say that?

Attraction.

The word fell out accidentally, right in the middle of the square. The tiny shadow of a bird flitted across the sand, he saw the risk of dying, I thought, in every woman. For him there was no »loss plus something else«, only finished. Ex, I said out loud.

Of course, there were more rounds without Mayakovsky. A child ran out of a house with a white satin bow in her hair, hopped along on one leg in front of us, one pure loosening-up.

Sure, he said. You're absolutely right.

I would have liked to make friends with the child. The thought shot through my head: this tiny Anita sitting in front of a broken mirror, weeping for the loss of her little bird. Distraught, she looks at her ripped dress, the mirror has torn it, on top of everything else. A smarter house with ghetto-type steps.

He wasn't called Vladimir. Was I called Anna then?

What makes you say that?

Despair. I almost said: let's talk about the weather. His hand was in my hand, that's not what it was about. He begged. Circular argument means that another's misfortune should stand for one's own. So help, Anna. Anna was eager not to be Anna.

Agreed? I said.

Tell me your plan.

Firstly, I is somebody different each time, you will be made happy in many different ways and the whole thing won't programmatically end in squalor.

Secondly? he asked meekly.

Each sets their own limits, athletic, the child reaches fifty hops wearing a Sunday dress.

Were these the main points? I said, no. Images of moments as they faced us. Always the momentary.

I'm all for a coffee, he said.

One last round.

We ended up in a small bar. I wasn't really with it, that is, my thoughts wandered between satin and jacket while he described Mayakovsky's yearnings: my precious, beloved and loveable Lily-child, not one single letter from you, you're not a kitten any longer, but a twisted screech owl. Etc. On the 21st I shall push off to the sea. Utterly yours, your Mexican puppy.

Touching, I said. And what's it got to do with me?

Pssst, he said. Push off into the universe!

Crazy.

I looked through the square of the window at a yellow ghetto house. Actually I listened to my heart beat.

When's it my turn?

Soon, precious, precious fox pup.

As though I were trapped in a Russian book. As though love could be conjured up with kitten-endearments and suchlike.

The canal was black. The seven o' clock twilight fell like night in the alleys. Vladimir didn't leave me alone. Why should he.

You realise of course, that as an educated man one cannot live without you.

Mayakovsky?

Original text, he said.

That's how you've done me out of futurism, the object of my journey.

Sorry, he said, but I'm serious.

I don't know how long we walked through the city. It was heavenly, with a hail of vulgar temptations. I'm a crocodile. When love grows fat it disturbs the sense of balance. Worrying, if two lovers had to decide whether the apocalyptic horsemen should be on their way or not. No dispossession. Love doesn't suffocate in personal ambition, it is itself the medium of suffocation. I control my naked life. Anti-love — the victim's standpoint (?). As a love-dissenter, I'm a self-destructive demi-fool who brings disaster to others. A few hops and jumps will still be needed. Don't supply a cartoon strip, no. Self-determination. There's a smog of sympathy which clouds clear-sightedness (deepest scepticism). Neither inside nor outside, neither here nor there: No-Man's-Land. Absence of solidarity makes me a wandering knight. Where does my state of emergency begin, if not here. I could even imagine a world-wide alliance of insistent fools. Common sense burns up in love's radiance. Give up. The animal in man makes use of every opportunity. Live with a budgie. At least behave as though the status quo were the most peaceful of all possibilities. Rather be the subject of my Fate. A decided bacheloress (presumptuous?), what does that have to do with poisonous bitch. Love must be put in its place. Two people — laughable.

We sat beside the canal and hung our feet in the water.

I — Communist and bear, Vladimir mumbled, already compromised by mistakes and over-enthusiasm.

Doesn't matter.

...Sought frail, slender, red-haired, large-eyed lady to hatch plans and polemicize.

Please, I said. At my house there are *rissoles* and intense interiors.

Beside ourselves with passion, we agreed to never part.

We

AND I LAID the angel on his back. The scenery towered above
    him.
These trees don't look so good, he said, but the side of the
    mountain is resting on exactly the right spot.
Who's resting? I asked.
Whoever you want, he said. You or me.
His face shone with the brightest colours.
Your hair, I said, feels like grass.
That's not it, he said. The sky's already turning grey.
Your hair, I said.
The sea, he said. I can hear it roaring.
You mean the mountain wind.
Well then you try it.
I held my face to his face. I buried myself in the blue of his eyes.
Well then, he said.
Well then the sea, I said. From one brightness to another.
Takes on shapes.
Am I above and below at once.

You are, he said, without your flat face above mine, quite
    unimaginable.
The sea, I said.
Don't change the subject.
I reminded him of the swallow summer, of the circling birds over
    the bay.
Mountain wind, he said.
I breathed on his hair.
You're forgetting, he said, the mountain's position. It can't do
    whatever it wants.
Can I?
The blue of his eyes darkened a degree.
You manage to cope with the sides at least.
And you, you're lying down.
He didn't deny it.
I remember, he said, how the swallows were circling. There was
    no escape.
The sea, I said.
No way out.
The evenings and the swallows, we got rid of them.
Sacrifice, he said. The sea roared.
Love me.
The tree is growing out of your face, he said. There are sick trees
    growing here. But yes.
But what?
If you want.
Do, I said.
He fixed his eyes on the cloud above the tree. He heard the sea
    roaring.
Now, he said.
Amore. Oh, the wind.
Your not-being-there.
That's how broken dreams are swept up.
With crowning hands.
Clearing away polar lights.
There will be no failure.

His barbed words bored into my ears.
Love, I said, a word from a dead language.
Wrong, he said in his dazzling way. You're lying on top of me.
Chaste or joined?
Both and, he said. Extremes are useless.
His tongue pressed into my mouth, instrument of a truly experi-
enced soul. We thought about the mountain.
Never, he said.
Up to the summit? I asked.
Quite unnecessary.
Your journey has already begun.
The sides, he said, facilitate a gentle ascent.
Through forest and scree.
He put his hand on my back.
Please, I said.
It was before the swallows, he said. I insisted on a love letter.
Of non-love.
I took the empty sheet to heart.
A brazen whiteness, veiling all rules. But please, I said.
But I'm looking at you.
The alphabet of looks, I said, lends itself to night. Don't ignore it.
That would make us friends.
I found him strange. Even if bitterness does make you inventive
— it still produces only meaningless meanings.
The sea, he said.
You're wrong.
You were never sociable.
I ran my hand through his labyrinth of hair. I kissed the mistake.
If at all, he said, then a really sensible illness. And life is neatly
passed by.
Allegorist!
He half started an attempt at seduction, right there under the oak
tree.
If you love me, he said, give the slogans a miss. Stumble into
your own ambiguity.
How calculating, I said.

Do it.

Tangle myself up in ambiguities, I said, your advice from last year.

Then kiss me.

I kissed the man or the woman and felt I was making a momentary oxymoron.

Impetuousness, he said, without impetuousness there is no embrace.

Then you want to inhabit me?

Of course. You are like deepest night to me.

He dared. Just as he turned down my request, I was ready to burn up in him.

Half sea, half mountain, he said.

Non-specific, for us.

That seems exaggerated.

You weave your way through the lie. You —

Oh, he said. He was lying down.

Had I wounded him? The angel was labyrinthine and, beneath the experience of his inverted love, neutral. He didn't suffer from any mask.

You're so cryptic, he cried. Omnipresent, unreachable.

Tell me about it.

For one-and-a-half ages you've ruled this tree.

I gave a shrill laugh. Mistress of an oak tree — how vulgar! And this tryst with a gong.

He took my hand. He didn't talk of love.

As though I'd already been and gone.

He was silent.

As though you'd filled the air with absence.

He put his arms around my waist.

You're my invitation, he said. Don't pretend you don't know.

I think I do know. You mean the return of night.

Exactly, he said. These tufts scratch your skin.

Heather.

Experience of night.

And all the tiny, tiny animals, dead or not.

I move towards you. Slowly I approach the bastion of the desert, the entrance before me.

And resume your hesitation.

As far back as I can remember, he's always been there.

Let's do it.

You want love.

Sublime destruction, no.

He refused to give the proper answer. He looked me up and down like a shameless, shrewd woman, quite literally carnally.

Whoever wants to touch you risks a capricious spirit.

Oho!

And while I studied his hair colour I longed for compassion.

The wind, he said.

Not again, I said.

You don't fool me.

He was chewing on an age-old hurt, neither malignant nor frivolous.

Am I annoying you? Well then.

He was lying down. The tips of his fingers were pressing gently into my neck.

It doesn't always have to be nothingness, I said. Non-human magnificence.

Half flesh, half skin and cartilage, he sang. Every woman is a Queen.

And you're not thinking of Heaven?

It's radiant with or without me.

There I sat, regally above, without expectation.

The crescent moon, he said, is exactly above the parting in your hair.

I don't know, I said. What's going on inside you? But still.

But still what, he said.

Let's do it.

I won't run away.

We formed a square. A bastion of the desert. We were without where-from and where-to.

Take me, he said.
I forgot the sea.
Take me, he said.
I forgot the mountain.
I ran my tongue over his face. Panting, I named him King of
Nothingness, of Duality, of Silent Cunning. And as the balls of
our thumbs rubbed together, he pushed inside. Like an
accomplice. Into a growing house.
Ah.
Yes, I whispered.
You.
Are the one.
His teeth sparkling, he marked me with his breath. Discarded his
sorrow in instalments. Now.
We seized it. I say: we. I say it out of neither hypocrisy nor
rhetorical precision. Night revealed the brilliance of our deed.

Rosa Aghios or
The Journey

MY THIRD ATTEMPT at an interpretation failed as well. It was not a teenage school girl with burning cheeks and indivisible desire who sat opposite me, but a Rosa from Friaul, half girl, half woman, servant in a great house. She stared out at the rugged landscape, murmuring "Ajax" from time to time and twiddling her thumbs. I thought she was in love or a little confused, but she gave more details. Home, yes, where there was a stone house and a garden of stinging nettles. There she would creep up on the rarest birds, would bury her arms in warm hay. There she would abandon herself to a hundred different thoughts, reading amongst the cabbage leaves. None of this concentrated light, she summed up, the sky is matt and my father limps.

Accident at work?

Feeding deer.

With these words her enthusiasm flagged. I saw Rosa cross an abandoned street with a civilian, the rows of firs, of pears and apples had not yet passed by while she accused herself of having hats instead of relatives.

Ajax.

Sorry?

Oh, that doesn't belong here. The rosy-cheeked deer roam particularly close to the house.

With equal aimlessness I relinquished myself to my thoughts. Here, Rosa, speckled like a rainbow trout, there a Doctor of Political Economy, between them a circle of knitting virgins — I pushed against the direction of travel, against all evidence, into my future behind me. Let's call it Trieste. Let's assume it's fed by a regular breaking of surf. Henchmen aren't henchmen, but gentleness and determination are also gone. And as I beg indulgence, the cape withdraws, exposing ever more compact views. Something like that.

I thought of Rosa again. Rivers that flow against the current are her favourite, the coast wind damages the ears and at the edge of any feasting you'll find Mr Excessive.

I nodded. How old could Rosa be, that she dragged Time along like a piece of string? After all, she was moving in the direction of travel and Friaul was where it was.

Rosa Aghios. The *tall, young, blonde woman with the sweet figure, only her hands showing the marks of hard work.* And Aghios shouted: *But why must my daughter lie beneath me like that? I don't want her. It's not my fault.* Deer feeding and a lemon-yellow book, only I didn't like to ask her. Rosa dozed with her thumbs in motion, as though she were grinding river sand.

In the dream, Mr Aghios's rotting face had lain against a vehicle. Beneath him endless space, above, the same. At Görz his dream began to relax. He let his head sink onto the upholstery, climbed into his own childhood and forgot the signorina. Instead he saw an empty field, a farmhouse and smoky light. He suffered no pangs of conscience, for he travelled towards his solitude. With that he also buried the legend of the double journey.

Rosa was sleeping. Or was she? In different lights her hands flickered up, her lap became a white apron and I felt I could make out Ajax, surrounded by the smell of herbs and cold. Time drives the past before it like jetsam, all silence is chatter, except your own name. Rosa Aghios. *Do you want me with you?* Mr Aghios pressed himself even more firmly against his vehicle so as to remain unseen. He travelled in a spaceship, in a gondola, in a barque, in the Görz-Trieste freight train. *I want my son not to stay alone.* After this opening Rosa asked: *And what should you do with your lack of freedom, if all around there is only enslavement?*

Rosa, Rosa. She dreamed animal dreams while the river, swollen with melt water frightened me from beyond the train window. The ice-grey water ran down to the valley floor. Constantly breaking its own shadow pattern and roughening the bank. Compared to that my surf broke gently.

Who's stumbling?

The horse, I whispered startled, as though I had to save Rosa's sleep. With sloping ribs.

She blinked. The nag, that's not good.

So things weren't looking too good in Friaul. I was just going to ask her about the abandoned street, about the civilian and the stillness entwined in green, but her gaze was caught by the swirling river.

Quite an epic, I said, to my own surprise.

Whatever, she replied calmly. The poor, poor horses. What I don't understand, is this confusion on earth and beyond.

Now was my moment to mention Mr Aghios's dream-space-ship, with which he had intended to escape this very confusion — there, Rosa, between Görz and Trieste —, instead I declared carelessly that it was a matter of altering boundaries.

And that's supposed to give direction?

Direction, yes.

Sideways or upwards?

Whichever you want.

It was hard to say whether Rosa was thinking of her master or of the edges of her valley. Her thumbs moved slowly, as though each movement checked off one more possibility.

Sideways, she decided, because I often feel hemmed in. Whole cliffs cave in and there's no escape.

The valley: the garden full of nettles, the snuffling pigs, barbed fences, deer feeding in the pine forests, further up rocky, then snowy peaks, oh yes, and the nags in their shafts along the abandoned street.

Rosa Aghios wore patent leather shoes. In the unpaved valley she was greeted and parted from simply. It happened so quickly that she couldn't remember ever having arrived. So was she dreaming upright, with Time undecided?

They dropped me. First misjudged, then pushed to the fore, then dropped. If you're going to dance to a stranger's tune, they said, then you can't expect to warm yourself in the snows of home.

Tired moss, I said. An epic in moss form.

I don't fiddle about now, I follow my chosen path.

Rosa had herself under control. What united us was our past future in Julian-Venice or wherever. I too had been dropped from the valley anti-patent-leather-shoe-club. Since then I've felt like talking about the sun.

A simple departure isn't worth discussing, she said.

And what do you do if two fatherlands lay claim?

As though caught red-handed she mumbled "Ajax" and that change had changed.

You're withholding your lover or the unknown soldier.

Rosa wasn't listening. Ajax was driving her in another direction and I realised it was too late for Mr Aghios. She had lured him into the trap of monogamy and absinthe.

Rosa with the emotional thumbs. Whispering, she vouched for something. And just as I wanted to ask her about her motherland, she complained that she felt hemmed in by my nervous feet.

Two roe deer.

Who for?

That would need considering.

I didn't have an Ajax, not even a home town that I could have suppressed. Who for then?

Are you trying to sit up again?

With my left leg, the right one wants to do something different.

And your self-esteem?

I forgave her the nosy question. There were rare days when I had some. On a windy February morning when nobody wanted anything from me, I carried my head higher. Then it seemed possible to alter everything, to keep animals with Egyptian confidence. And a canary whistled in the square of my dreams.

Inside herself she could only hear voices saying no, although she still kept on working towards the edges, towards these eastern borders, towards this Friaul nonsense. Oh yes, I am not called Hortense and my parents are not advantaged! Her voice cracked. Welcome and it's all over!

It was only now that I noticed her eyes were changing colour and that our union was already advanced. From the heights of his journey, Mr Aghios had recognised the domestic pet in man, Rosa extinguished herself more and more, that made her strong. One day there she would be with a new name, on the plains.

I forgot the imagined rifts and my reasons for walking into the sea. Be forgotten as quickly as possible, red collar turned up and better uphill than downhill.

I only mean that we need a more powerful proposal.

Just don't reveal any meeting-places!

That's one of my ground rules.

Rosa's eyes shone.

There are too many cupboards in the house and the street has gone to pot.

Don't worry.

The dust causes nausea and coughing.

Whatever.

I didn't want to hear any more about the missing paddocks, after all you don't have to abandon yourself to a village where the thatch is loose.

Rosa Aghios twiddled her thumbs gratefully. Her speckled face showed the first hint of a smile.

I'll tell Rosalie.

Good.

And I showed her the *flurry of light*.

Pitterman, listen

To have enough fear.

Ilse Aichinger

EVENING. A FAINT LIGHT fell through the crack in the door, I was lying down and the trains were already screeching. Beyond the deserted garden the engines gasped, carriages clattered on the sidings, between it all metallic screams. In the darkness the steel giants drew closer and closer, the wheels, the whistling, I cried out, I was four: is the room still there? The faint strip of light was still there, a quivering track along which the Unknown rode in, pushed in, clanking and groaning. I was surrounded.

He pulled me out of my paralysis, Pitterman with the assyrian beard and the sparkling eyes. Uncle Pitterman, who appealed to my pride. Scared? His deep voice drowned out the rattling and howling, his hand settled on my forehead and despair retreated. Retreated back beyond the garden, crept away into the heavy metal of the buffers, stayed there, militant. Did not return to the black cube of the room. They shunt desperation back and forth, I thought, and thought about the assyrian beard. Which, upright, plunged me into sleep.

November afternoon. The relaxing of concentration, the empty cemeteries, the cawing of the crows above the forest. *The chains pull tighter. We must be more agile, so that before heaven the game remains ever the same. Growing older in this sense, means learning to play better.*

In the mirror I examine the two vertical wrinkles on my forehead, the tea is having no effect, apprehension remains. I think of the imminent extravagance of Christmas presents (nonsense, nonsense), of the loneliness that will follow. Of Oscar's heavy, fleshy face. Herta coughs dangerously, Marta almost invisible, Ingrid doesn't know up from down. Baby boom yes, but no daily-bread-art. Fast beats the pulse in the throat.

Snow would bring calm now. Snow on the branches, the mosses, the black asphalt. On my son's plate-shaped cap. Swiftly oblivion sinks over all things. The Jewish purification water, the Russian over-boots are at rest. Only the neighbour's cat whines on, while I win back my sad composure.

Gurus do not guarantee freedom from fear. Tiny guards step out of the dream's grandfather clocks, chase about the room cracking whips.

First voice: A heavy charge has been brought against you.

Second voice: You will have to answer for yourself.

Third voice: You are under arrest.

Me: I am in your power.

Equipped with all the powers of state security officers, the guards could be called: Pyotr Nikolayevich, Nikolay Petrovich, Sergey Sergeyevich. At dream-speed they finish the thing off. Hup, two, three, four and you're in the jug. Innocent as always. *The mice twirl their long mustachios. And the cockroach Tarakan Tarakanovich crouches on the stove in a red-collared shirt, axe in hand.*

Exit all characters.

City, sinewed, sexy, solvent, successful, not scared of heights is what one should be and instead is plagued by migraines and claustrophobias. Skull, lift, cinema, aeroplane, are close, breath runs out. Jump out! Just stay away. Leave the pain alone, in the middle of the night. But there is this sticky spittle and the *construction* which allows no escape.

I ask for a winding path.

Air! Air!

In a Hassidic dance-step right out of all interpretations.

Come on, Sonny, burn the Japanese screen for me!

Beneath the carrot-red sky, beneath a wispy dawn.

Come on, come on !

Get rid of measurables, locks and bolts, disabilities, cots.

Drift sand.

Defiant, the little boy says someone should stick a plaster over the whole universe. Someone should stop the growth of this great Moloch who frightens and terrifies. He says and shakes his child's fist.

Fear of space, fear of closeness — in the blackness of the child's room at night these fears converge. As if one were being forcibly sucked away or were lying under a heavy stone. The accomplices of Evil lurk everywhere, whether in tails or not. Nothing is safe now, not even breath, it catches. Self is a double being, perhaps already dissolving. How can you be certain of your Self, how?

This is where panic sets in, the first cry for help. Who am I, where, who will tell me?

Not the witches and dead grandmothers and burglars and policemen, not the crazy stars and built-in cupboards and not the skinny animals, not the rustlings and squeakings, the shadows and snakes, no. What is so terrifying is the lost Self. The threat of emptiness. All around, all around.

The child: Pitterman, is that you?

Pitterman: Hold onto my beard.

The child: I'm holding onto it already, otherwise I'd float away.

Pitterman: The buildings collapse and everything empties.

The child: No!

Pitterman: The walls of the houses plunge into the seas.

The child: No, no!

Pitterman: A birdie in your head, and a froggie in your bed.

The child: Stop it, uncle.

Pitterman: When it's night-time, animals come, winged, just for us.

The child: No.

Pitterman: Sleep now, little lonely one, sleep.

That's what it was like when the voice and the beard put the world back in order, the world which had got messed up. Over there in the East, sometime after the war.

Pittermen must come, for mothers and children, with a dependable assyrian beard. Pittermen against the spinning world of terror. Pitterman!

Pletnyov or Unpairable

What's wrong, my wife? It began so well,
must it now end badly?
Alexander Pushkin to Natalia Pushkina

WEEPING. EVER since the final dissolution of the relationship,
Pletnyov has wept. It can't be because of the snow. The snow is
falling sleepily, softly on entwining stillness. And yes. The snow
is white. White and light like two clouds in the sky, that was how
they'd once drifted together. Pletnyov weeps. Pah! to the snow,
pah! to everything everywhere. Bile bothers him. Where does
Anna nibble those "October" biscuits now? With whom? God be
with her, or rather: not with her. I'm not putting my head back in
that noose, not of my own free will.

The nightmares told, then Andreyeva: Who's tormenting
you? The angel left long ago. Nights too long. Pletnyov begs pity.
He does it with perfectly coiffured hair, neatly dressed and with
a wry look, but his director, grief, forbids his losing himself in
another's eyes. Am I a person without moral sense? Andreyeva
sees him as one of the most heroic of victims. A certain Masha

offers him a calming tea. Weeping he confesses to being anti-family, from Monday to Friday: Me! Excessive enthusiasm and every possible opportunity to retreat. At the height of the storm he watches for wild geese and blindly aligns himself with disorder. Hunted, misjudged, forgotten, yes sir! A tiny, cheated boat that runs aground on the hidden reef of inconceivability. I can-not be-lie-ieve you love me, I can-not be-lie-ieve you're true. Masha examines Pletnyov's hairless eyebrows, which glisten in the light. Oh no, no, why the swan song? Pletnyov weeps on: even the wild geese are out of their minds and Masha, that tropical butterfly from Jakutsk, can't talk him out of his decision to constructively, methodically, positively, cerebrally renounce woman.

Andreyeva: Why are you being so dreadfully dramatic? That's how Indian chiefs talk.
Pletnyov: If you think so. I'll stagger out into the corridor in a minute. Every special subject has it's own particular depth. It's just that you still don't know who I am.
Andreyeva: Like you say, a special subject.
Pletnyov: Why so cheeky? Am I supposed to be worse than that snow-king who's measuring you up with his eyes?
Andreyeva: Be quiet.
Pletnyov: All right, I'm going.
Andreyeva: See these balls?
Pletnyov: What balls?
Andreyeva: Slowly mankind is losing form and becoming a ball. And once a ball, losing all desire.
Pletnyov: Heard it before. Dreadfully dramatic.
Andreyeva: Sorry?
Pletnyov: Just that. Where's my coat?
Andreyeva: In the dovecote.
Pletnyov: Madame is sneering.
Andreyeva: Not at all. The soup is getting cold.
Pletnyov: Obviously a *cul-de-sac*.
Andreyeva: Three o' clock at the zoo then.

Anna knows her Marx. In church she feels herself to be simply an annoying appendage. She acts according to her own judgement, quickly and painlessly. Two bright blue eyes shine out beneath the peak of a modest hat. She thinks of thin ribbons of smoke above the villages, of jackdaws. The painting will always have an amateurish beauty, she knows, and that she has a thing about nature. A sadness remains for the dog that had crept into the bushes to die. A quite animal, positively unrestrained, spontaneous sympathy. I don't need any special terms! Anna glows when she's hastening after the shadow of a melancholic. The evening sky glows. Five times she has been bridesmaid and five times been to a masked ball. She can answer existential questions, not just a: get yourself out of your own mess. In a hop, skip and a jump she is beside the confused friend, shakes her short hair and listens. Then the thoughts flood back: *they* sat there…They, Anna and Pletnyov. On the flat beach with the little puddles. Pletnyov's ninety-five faces reflected in the water. Who is this man?

Tell me who you are. Are there still as many women in love with you? He dismisses her question as scandal. O woe, youth is long gone. And a screw is not a nail. Anna wants to see a miracle and sees none. She is standing on the stony traffic island, staring into the blackness of his jacket. She has never been humble. Kolyenka, I'm going to fly. And the sardine tin falls from her hand. At home in the frost, the faded heads, the tiny surgical knives. Everything has "been", background, alienation, oh, oh, oh. The clock ticks its penetrating, soft tick. Be careful not to get drunk, darling, she says and can't sleep a wink. Love rushes past her. Struck, shattered. She opens her mouth wide from the pain. Then everything moves very quickly. She turns around and marries nobody.

Masha easily grasps his double game. If he's complaining about Andreyeva, then she's the Tea Queen; if he praises the other, then she's the one left standing. Then he comes back from the zoo, damaged and seeking shelter in her frills. So sweet for weeping in. Should she smile, or disappear rustling into a dark corner? Her eyes are small, like bird's eyes, but bright. Whenever she meets children on the street she plays with them. Guardian angel of the light-footed. As though her salvation were dependant on a ball and wiry, young rebels. Pletnyov suspects her of only being happy with such juveniles. Fine down grows above her lips, she spent her childhood under cloud swarms in the Tundra. Masha's shapeliness, her big heart, her firm belief in superstition.

Masha, do me a favour and get rid of that frightful kitchen clock.

But no! She loves being under the spell of that imp with hands in the shape of a knife and a fork. She dreams of numbers and then adds them together. 77 is quite prepared to throw itself, with her — head over heels — into eternity.

Masha, where does this belated self-confidence come from?

Oh, stop it, puzzle-man.

As a cancerian, Pletnyov appears cobalt blue to her, he entered her life by chance, when the sum of her age was 7. The stars predict happiness, only Pletnyov won't accept it. She's hurt. Sometimes her face grimaces and her lips murmur something. My God, what a bastard. Should she go over and find out what's really wrong with him *there?* Lie in wait for the nice lady? How disgusting. No, I won't do it. No, I won't do it. I'd rather drink Vodka.

Lonely, Pletnyov sits at his desk staring at Niobe. Wretched paperweight. Now that he believes himself immune to woman's tentacles he wishes it in hell. Masha is soothing, Andreyeva is sobering, but this figurine… Pah, how silly. He will replace it with a cube. He's still capable of inspired writing. Down with sleep! I'm going to write continuously for seventeen hours! His whole body is shivering with impatience. From desk to cupboard, from cupboard to desk. *Marriage is a deadlock… and then you die without having done one single miracle in your life.* The sun is shining straight into his eyes. He screws them up and lights a pipe. What peace. At a wave of his hand *they* would all come

37

running, but he doesn't want them. No and no again. He will go to Kaluga alone and turn the country hovel into a glorious brick house. No moodiness and half-heartedness — action and awakening awareness! A pretty good career.

A knock.

Pletnyov: Who's there?

Masha: You're in emptiness today, or am I mistaken?

Pletnyov (grinding his teeth): You're mistaken.

Masha: The day is greeny-blue, a twenty-fifth...

Pletnyov: Don't give me all that mysticism.

Masha: An invitation to tea, then.

Pletnyov: As though you wanted to invite me to a drinking party.

Masha: I'm heavy with sleep.

Pletnyov (whining): How's anyone supposed to understand this?... Come in.

Wanda and Johann

AS LITERARY ADVISOR she had a language assistant to help her. You're so petty, he said, always *interfering in some detail*. She talked to him. Write, he said. From time to time he quoted from Rousseau's key theory that man is fundamentally good. Fundamentally, she repeated and took a sip of ginger tea. He had read his way through Locke, Buckle, Kant, while for her the Island Sea was taking shape, setting for an atrocity. The seagulls, she said. He read. The seagulls are offending against sovereign rights over territorial waters, Johann! — No system at all, was Buckle's solution. — The seagulls, she said. Should be destroyed. He was silent, she pulled at her petticoat. A strategy for dealing with seagulls and the sea lavender will blossom once more.

Who she was? His fiancée. When they intended to marry? *In summer, of course.*

The seagulls led them to Copenhagen and back to the island P. The man responsible lived from advances — a tramp, a poet, a cocainist. In his solitude he chose his own spiritual diet. She gave him sand-dunes and a leaden sea. A faded sun and seagulls' cries. He left himself stranded on the beach. Johann slept. He hadn't ruffled her with Buckle. Slowly she had intensified the storm and it now swept over P., making the marram grass bend in the wind and the seagulls drop like stones, white foam. Solitude faces you with self-appraisal. He ran across the island, back and forth, wearing a woollen hat. Beyond a pine the sea's horizon. And he cursed negation.

Do you have to, said Johann. — What? — *Seek out your heart with a knife if you have no control over your own destiny.* — The seagulls, she said, crown witnesses, I see. — Seagulls, sea-lions, how comic! The house stood in the open, right in the middle of the heath, they chose this respectable man, tie or no tie, he provided the best target. — They circled him, they pecked him, they… — Disgusted, he turned away. And night sank over the island landscape.

The next day she bled in a red rage so the *twenty-nine girl-friends tiptoed* along her corridor bringing tablets and teas. Anton, she said, but nobody knew who she was talking about. The light in the room was gentle. She stared at the white floor-tiles, called them ocean and her language assistant a "Buckler." Buckle is driving God out of him, she complained. There remains just a *shovelful of chatter.* Wasted words, whispered a friend in her ear. Air, light, let's leave this philosophical thicket! Evening found her alone. Sitting up in bed, leaning against some pillows and staring at the Island Sea. The coastline ran straight, the sand was the colour of straw.

In eight days there will be a death, said Johann. Your seagulls will have done the deed. She wrote. She gave a short cry and advised him to use a mirror for his neck. The Enlightenment has done nothing for you. — And what should a view of my neck teach me? He was very confident. He took a piece of paper and drew the sea with such a huge horizon that you could see the earth's curve. He drew a second sea with a buoy painted white. He drew a third sea with the shore in the foreground and a few *bald skerries* further out. Then she hugged him and suggested a steamer trip.

They reached the steamer at a run. Water slapped over the deck. Promise me you won't read my book, she said. The contours of the pines on the bank were like the contours of clouds, he showed that to her. Promise, she called into the wind. I'm not mad quite yet, shouted Johann, I can still *bring forest and island into harmony with my innermost feelings*. He leaned against the deck railing. The bank faded, dirty-white gulls screamed on the deck, and with his love of life grew also the desire to touch the back of his fiancée's head. With her eyes closed she murmured: Tea. Wanda, he said, that's not appropriate. Is standstill the law? Ginger tea, she added. So the steamer sailed on around the lake, with fluttering pennants, crown-witness-seagulls and a little music, while at the railing all was as it had been. Johann had promised nothing and Wanda was inflamed by P.

Below her was the spruce wood, *cheek by cheek like an army*, beyond it the sea broke along the shore and beyond the waves stood naked islands of rock, like a whole fleet of armoured ships. That was how she saw it through tramp's eyes. What do you think of a shipwreck? Johann's morale had sunk low, she had him *under the soles of her boots*. A ship wrecked between skerries — if you want. A drunken, royal navy pilot would manage it, no problem. Just leave your go-under-man out of it. She giggled. She sketched the aft salon and Johann fled into the café. Certainty begins in doubt, Buckle knew. Buckle was right. For Truth was relative and might *lie on either side*.

Wanda suggested bicarbonate of soda and linguistic research. Since the shipwreck she had been humming to herself; sea-pilots had replaced the seagulls, word-revolutions, sulked Johann, but to speak of his feelings was pointless. P. was made of light, grainy sand. Once the sand was warmed by the hot summer sun, it did not cool down again at night. The cocainist warmed his lung with hot sand bags. The cocainist trudged through the deep sand — one step forwards, half a step back —, feeling he was sinking through the earth *like the girl that walked on bread*. Without a fixed point, without —

— at the risk of landing on his island a corpse. Low tide! called Wanda. — Your old man should go fishing, shipping. Johann misspoke and promised: not a line of it will I read. Have you ever fished for perch? she asked. He thought of Buckle and a bathing place. Impertinent, he replied that he didn't know, that he only knew she grew daily more intrusive. Until that other reunion *there*.

Wanda's hell was perfect. Her investment swam off. At the question "When?" there fell a short "Now!" like the crack of a whip over draught cattle.

For hours she stood on the balcony and stared at the clouds. Obsession as punishment, she whispered until her ears were assailed by so many minute noises. P. no longer began at the edge of the forest. Johann had removed it. The heath, the beach, the coast-line, *the empty space closed about her person*.

Monday: ate dates, Tuesday: ate dates, on Wednesday, using cyan-blue ink on wax-cloth, she wrote: "*I had my scene.*"

After all, this is solitude: *to spin yourself into the silk of your own soul*, to create your own cocoon and wait for the change. Seagulls circled the house on the heath and the cocainist spoke the word "*chrysanthemum*" aloud. A question mark in his intonation. In the lamplight Wanda saw the man at the chrysanthemum-table, herself beside him with the child who belonged to neither of them. Child! He went, he returned home to his solitude, *there I sat, with everything behind me, everything*, the choice between him and him.

From time to time the girl friends stayed away for days on end; she grew gloomy and ran to exchange silver for copper. She couldn't get the child out of her mind. How had *he* managed it? Out of grief for his possible double-life she sketched a cliffy coast-line with chalky rocks, rugged like a reef. The child glowed. How had *she* managed it? Yesyes — yesyes — yes — ye-es. Cocainist *et fils*. Her cape was caught by the wind and struck her face.

That man pulls himself up yet again! With *"Marmelade russe"*, fifty volumes of poetry, while my own life begins out at sea. The dunes shone wanly, the bays were filled with silt, no good for the child, no good. First she was overcome by a trembling, then, with a gesture of deliverance, she swept the paper from the table and took herself off to the northernmost edge of the town.

And?
    Fine, thanks.
    P.?
    Excellent.
    News?
    The newspapers did that.
    What are you anyway?
    And Buckle?
    She took his hand, which had never told her anything, and read the child's dreamed future.

The Door to the Sea

AND I THOUGHT it would be easy to describe. The sea below me. Blue, no, white, no, green, no, one with the sky, no, ruffled, no, smooth, no, all that and still more. How to capture motion. It's so beautiful. I don't try.

The first time, I took the path by the baroque steps, steep, but quick. I crossed Jesuit Square, children were riding their bikes here between gravel and grass, even the trees unsightly. I made my way towards the edge. I reached the curved wall and stood in its shadow. I walked along the wall, across an improvised football pitch, the children make do with only a few metres, just let me through. The path narrows, one step, a second and wherever can this pine get its water from, growing right out of the stone. The black paling door. It's open. This must be it. I step through the opening in the wall and see it all around me in brilliant brightness, flowing and free I could touch — jump! The sea. I sat down on the small plateau and looked. Nothing but that. I shut my eyes, it was there, it thundered on the rocks far below.

Then, with the heat, the women came out one after the other in black or patterned aprons, in slippers, crept out of the shady houses and sat down in the sun. Their voices drowned out the breakers. A murmuring carpet spread over a shimmering sea. They were used to the sight. They had deaths to discuss, knitting patterns, too. They talked themselves up into higher pitches. I searched the haze for the Montenegro mountains. Nothing to be seen. I left.

The second time I took Neda with me. This time not up the steep steps, but along "Hades" street. She laughs, as though this were the perfect street for her. Above the sea she doesn't laugh any more. She stares at it fixedly. And? The blue. And? I can't bear its beauty. Yes, I say. There's something, she says, that you don't know about. We look at the sea. I had a son, she says, he died.

I stroke her red hair, the white sticking-out ears, helpless. Clinical death, twice, she says, heart. Whose heart? Mine, she says. The child was born, it died four weeks after birth. Neda, I say.

The sea lies like a sheet of plastic below us, a self-absorbed element.

No, she says. Never. The doctors said never.

For your sake.

What do I matter. They can't guarantee the baby would be alright. But that —

Yes.

For three months she hadn't been able to talk about it with anyone. For three months she had sat in her flat as though turned to stone, crying. Life had divided into Before and After. She hadn't been able to join the two ends ever again. One Neda comforts the other, encourages her. Nobody knew anything about that.

What is it about the beauty that hurts? I ask.

She still stares at the sea.

The memory, she says. In that darkest tunnel, colours lit up, indescribable. Death.

We heard no sea, no gossiping women, the sun was in the west, copper-red, Neda's plait burned, I pushed her up to the railings, no, she screamed, not face to face! and darted backwards through the door. There, look at the blue mountains, I said, conciliatory. But she made her way down to the underworld, Hades street, do you understand now?

The third time I went alone, to escape the crowds of tourists. I slipped through the opening in the wall, the wind swept into my face. Quarrelsome sea. I had never thought abyss, but now I did. And my thoughts wandered back to the Jesuit church which was decorated with sweet carnations for the Risen Lord. The railing was of almost no use at all. Soared high into the heavens, but left and right anything was possible, anything. I closed my eyes. I waited for the women's voices. I wanted them to be there. Someone came. I looked up. An adolescent came and lay down on the stone with the inscription "free". I didn't ask whether he was cold. I opened the book and read:

He has probably fallen asleep. The shadow of the hedge covered the whole square of the future terrace. M. found himself in its shelter without any memory of his gradual movement. He must have fallen asleep again and again. The shadow of the hedge denser than any wall... He had neared the abyss for nothing. Never again, never again would he do that.

He slept. The other one, that one over there, freed, sea-like, adolescent, he slept. Why was I reading. Surely I wasn't ashamed that he stole my view. Neda's courage had deserted me in the face of this enormity, the sea.

Then came the first one, the second one, the old woman: oh Madame, back again! And why in black, in mourning perhaps? No, I say, thank you, no. And the second: you know, fashion. And the old woman: do you come from far away? Quite far, I say. Then, she says, have a good journey and laughs.

It was not the last time. I encountered the sea in the port, in the fishing bay, but only there behind the door, far below the walls, was it that sea. Mine. Neda had gone away. Mira was afraid of nothing. She said: show me the sea. I led her without any trouble across the football field, I pushed her through the door. She glowed and was silent. She sat down where Neda had sat, with her back to the sun, looking at the sea. Gentle, she said, I know the Pacific. I asked myself who she was. Can't she express her fear? And could I? I pointed to her belt: a plastic knife won't help much. She laughs. Or perhaps it will? Belts, I say, give you

46

security. You tie yourself in, the wider, the better. Of course, she says. I didn't say: Amazon. I only thought that this delicate body was denying its delicateness. Compulsion? I asked gently. I want it like that, she said, I'm practising resistance. While she carried on being mysterious the sun wandered westwards. The women were already perching on the rocks and knitting. Mira paid no attention to them, she asked: are you lonely? Her eyes lit up cheekily, I didn't understand. Forget it, she said. Whatever, I said, how should I know right out of the blue like that. You just are, she said. I admitted defeat.

We stopped talking. I examined her profile, she examined the sea. In this way the afternoon passed. The swallows began to circle. I asked myself who she was. And out of despair or out of love I opened the book.

I have bought a house, I read. *The area is very beautiful. It could be Greece. The trees which surround the house belong to me. One of them, gigantic, creates such a lot of shade, that I will never again suffer from the heat. I want to build a terrace. In the evening the lights of D. can be seen from this terrace...*

Here there are moments of a perfect, varied yet precise light which settles on one object, passionately...

The sea, she said.

You, she said.

I took her hand and we left the plateau. It had been the last time.

Walking

We can only live in the open, precisely
on the dividing line between light and
dark. But we are pushed irresistibly forwards. Our entire being aids and accel-
erates this urge.

René Char

I

THE PATH IS DUSTY and white. The sun glitters. Bright butterflies sway in the air. Rosemary, lavender and thyme exude the
smell of the south. Brittle broom and vineyards of poison green.
Your eyes look up — oh, these lush paths — look down. Sluggish
steps raising tiny dust clouds. Chalk dust. The blossoms on the
abundant bushes are blue. Every time your eyes look up, what a
blueness. And sweat seeping from every pore. Afternoon.
Sometime. Behind the tennis court is Somewhere and Sometime.
The road, like a white ribbon, leads. Away. Not to the farm, not
up the hill, but through it. Through a valley, self-sufficient. Steps
unhurried. Your gaze sweeps and rests. Broom stalks, as tall as a
man — your hand feels them. Smooth. The light, indefinable. So

your eyes close for a short, black moment. Your steps hesitate, as though the stones were stirring beneath the soles. All that counts is your foot that feels about in the desired direction. Already it's gone off the path. Eyes shut and straight into the thistles. Zigzag of blindness. The afternoon light glitters. Sparkling air, but keep walking, walking. Between wild kitchen-herbs, bushes, untiring. Eyes growing dimmer, a spotted butterfly stands out, a dragonfly. Motion keeps you going. And thoughts without anchor. Chinese koans are like that. All sides open, search for meaning. A slap in the face. The heat beats down. Thought cowers, feels the emptiness (or the reason for walking), your hand the broom stalks. In the head's chamber no paths, the black wolfhound barks tonelessly. Let everything split at the seams. Up there a sheep is grazing, if »up« is the right word. Through the valley as thoughts pass through and every possible thing is see-through. The dragonfly's wing. Is someone waiting? The hawthorn could be something from childhood. Sat under a bush with a Jonathan, with a Marika. But keep walking, walking. Your steps don't falter. Now you've become a fringe figure in the valley, a nameless passer-by. What's Privas? Knowing doesn't help. Why these stunted holm-oaks? The wood cools. Birds sing. Maintain this state of namelessness, here, later, everywhere. In the Between. Brown oak leaves from last year, and miserable the stream. In the head's *camera obscura* decay lies disconnected beside silenced speech. I does occur, but *en passant*. An I of shifting relations, passing through. Disconnected, silenced speech, right, while the light indicates a stone, the salamander an old dream. Keep going! The heat is beating down. Breath comes heavily, no wood now, what good is sun protection factor six. Shoes full of chalk dust, that cricket chirps without shame, with numbing regularity. Water would be nice. A daring desire with this fear of making an anagram of the situation. Of the non-situation. Stopping is part of motion too. Your hand feels a sticky leaf, that, when crushed, smells strange. The departure was abrupt. To the tennis court and beyond, losing sight of the hill in the side valley. Throw away security, follow the ribbon of the road, the horizontal urge.

Now-time. The broom stalks whip back, walking has wearied to ritual. Great grey-blueness in which off and on a detail shines out, a glaring thought. Of dropping out, of Marika's downy upper lip. The seams! From busy to *cogito*, search in vain for meaning. With sharpened pencil rip the paper, tickle ambition. But the dreams are decaying, decaying. While the heat beats down mercilessly. Your will, disarmed, floating, your left foot has given way. Is anyone offended? For miles quite alone among see-through dragonflies. The snake is still to come.

II

I CARRIED ON walking even as I lay. As I lay ill, horizontal, looking out at the distant hills through a tiny square window. The pattern of the vineyards and orchards and on a rounded hilltop, the heavenly Jerusalem. Méthamis. Instead of the snake, a scorpion appeared. A shy, black creature that disappeared into the darkest corner, its sting drawn. I slept or dozed, in feverish dreams I walked my feet to shreds. Even now still walking. Beneath the nomad's star which has scattered Jonathan, Marika and me, the Pannonic prowlers, in all directions. Are we suffering from the original text? From the most insipid to the most intense thoughts: ever and ever along the edges, without a centre. Collapsed into the bedclothes, with a craving for tea, silenced speech. My sluggish body won't respond, my head chirps, whirs. A fluttering flag? I translated three lines of Char, bore them across into the house of German grammar. Fell asleep. Dreamt, not a place, but a rushing stream of pictures. With that sharp slap in the face, which the Master unexpectedly bestows. Koan, or the after-effects of shingles. Marika's carrot-red hair in the airstream, and the white chaos as we scattered. To find no cover. To drift out of the way with faultless rifts. Until the broom stalks whip back. And from the innermost centre of the bush,

50

absolute black peers out. The world, the broader context, I can't grasp it. People who lay claim to a piece of ground, are of a different type. Marika slipped through. The road is leading through. Through. Infinitives are only a feeble comfort, but at least they're open. The hills shone ochre-brown in the last light of the sun. My temperature rose to 39.2. France Culture discussed the difficulties of translation. They don't let themselves be dug out like weeds, they strike back with masculine rhymes. One must keep pushing through, without ever arriving. A couplet by Char, and the hills were blue. Bluey-purple. And Méthamis a Christmas tree. The hour of swallows, of non-hairsplitting. Marika disappeared with a jerk from memory, she had run off on soft Pannonic soles. Into her land of In-Between. Where did the ribbon end? The central strip of grass? I was still running. Into the valley, to the chalk quarry, my own helper in flight. Ran, although the wolfhound was tied up. Ran, or slept already. One and the same motion. Neither ending nor endless. No arriving please.

Lineation

WITH thought comes the softest of pinks.
I. Just differently phrased
You have left yourself, the light fal-
and more condensed.
ling into the room rests on the paper,
2. The world as will
nothing, which could not be considered,
and idea disappears
you have left out the edge, the
as in fog.
left-hand margin, the first
3. Counts, whatever is aroused
stroke can just as well be
and thinks.
vertical as horizontal as diago-
4. The inner need
nal. The grain in the paper. Hush.
of man lies outside
Just a lizard over the balcony
of him.

railing, five bars, that seems
                    5. *Lightning elucidation and*
fairly certain, five lines with a pale
                    continued search.
grid of shadows, tentative, your hand tests
                    6. *All inner processes*
its position, playing,
                    as words, take on
you let it all depend on the first
                    form.
touch of the paint on the
                    7. *The clotting of the early morning*
paper. Rippling, the sheet absorbing,
                    light, the simmering white
not stabile, not labile, you have
                    excitement.
begun. Have you begun?
                    8. *Excitement blazes without*
Brick-red runs the stroke and
                    aim or reason.
again: brush down,
                    9. *And goes out.*
brush up. Watered down, you could
                    10. *How to perpetuate it?*
say, the brick red. Hush, you
                    11. *By returning to poten-*
say. The paint has already
                    tiality, which knows no
thinned after all, vanished you'd
                    masks.
like best of all. The idea of an
                    12. *The eternity of movement,*
idea or an opaque white, no,
                    the movement of eternity.
the third bar, you draw the
                    13. *Everything open there!*

line, indifferent, a brush stroke,
        14. And simple assumption.
nothing more. Five, your hand has
        15. The appearances jump
decided. Arrived in pink,
        from excitement to excitement,
you hurry paleness forward.
        from origin to origin.
Fixed, freed in this
        16. An eternal circle
routine. For the fourth you reach
        of meaninglessness.
out with the brush, it finds its own way.
        17. The givings of meaning (legion)
The colour has become quite delicate,
        disappear into nothing
a hint on the paper, you don't renew
        after they have caused great
it for the last stroke, so
        ripples (cultures).
that the grid turns into a grid
        18. Endlessly meteors, suns,
of shadings, strength and red
        planets, comets chase
won from the first beginning which
        through the human head.
nurtures all that follows. Every line the
        19. Thought moves,
outflow of the one before, right back
        excitement doesn't.
to the beginning. Begun by
        20. And yet, mobile
the lizard, meant to say by the mo-
        thought won't admit that
ment of its disappearance, by the re-
        the 'firm foundations' are but

54

membered lizard. Hush. Where nothing
        trickling sand.
else is something comes to be, you open yourself
        21. Reality: 'real-
to this risk, to the
        ity'.
potential in your hand. Hush. The
        22. The reality of a snail
light falls onto the paper, the light
        is our sense of it.
could also not fall onto the pa-
        23. Torn away into
per, between the five lines
        distances and their excitement, where
another light modulating,
        face and mind fade.
here there is neither right nor wrong.
        24. The essence of man.
Lineature. Meant to say, you get to
        Where?
the bottom of these transitions. But they
        25. His psychomania for
are on top, the colour
        'useful' things (cabbage,
flows out. The exercise breaks off.
        pickles, cars).
Grid without a rush-hush-animal,
        26. A burning match
the purest play of light. Equally carefully
        shakes you up.
you would have forgotten a siskin,
        27. Rhythm — origin of all
creating bird-tininess
        origins.
in a colour-spit (spot splash). In
        28. Or excitement as

flight! After all we do want (do we?)
immaterial centre
to live forever. Hush. Long live
of a rotation.
self-denial. Eye-feelers,
29. That would make what is
hand, they achieve it. In the morning
called matter a system of movements
the hand is clumsy, but it leads
of powers, now moving
you, itself, to small epiphanies.
closer now further apart.
Lurches across the sheet and draws
30. Density of movement instead of 'substance'.
along its own shadow. You
Balance of power
see the meandering figure. It
instead of 'material'.
reminds you. You don't ask about
31. In a state of whiteness, movement
the creator. One and the other
reaches its greatest intensity
always fits. The brush circles,
and atomises.
the spiral advances into unknown
32. Neither nothing nor growth:
territory, always you are blame-
dynamic of excitement.
less. Absent? At the edges of
33. Does man even know
day that isn't a question. And you don't
how he could recognise
hesitate to extend the spi-
his atomised being in the cosmos?
ral tail-like with a blue
34. Everybody is, in his own way,

stroke of water-colour. The creation

not quite in his right mind.

stays small. A shadow of.

35. Non-mind, not-knowledge,

A short flaring up (of colour, form,

non-objectivity,

sense). You have - what? - brought it

not-boundary.

forth. The not-intention shines

36. For the universe has neither

out of the wave-shaped path of the

a roof that could be torn off, nor

lines, out of zigzag, out of soft shadow

a foundation that could be blown up,

and blurring dot. All around

nor walls which could be

is that which you are. White expanse, in-

knocked down.

different, no, set vibrating by

37. The coloured,

a hump, a hole, a hill

the black excitements.

of colour, by a disappearing tri-

38. But everything yearns

angle. Insular brick-red rises, your not-

towards the state of whiteness.

intention condenses in the

39. (Towards the highest geometry

paint. No centre, no dif-

of the conscious.)

ference, the paper reddens. Creates

40. The assumed sense

an arched bud, a tiny

of every connection is

fierce, un-fierce rebellion. Immediate,

proved wrong by chance.

57

yet long prepared. Up-stroke
        41. Nature acts in the triumph
down-stroke. The difference made
        of light, which illuminates
by something else so long before. Psst, it's
        its senseless movements
gone, the little lizard. The surge,
        in infinite darkness.
the oscillation. You hold nothing.
        42. Composure.
Nothing holds you. You examine the
        43. If perfection existed,
edges of the paper. The quivering
        it would get caught in a desert
shadow-rabbit on the table top. Whatever
        or move through
is produced, is already gone. The
        infinity
hand reaches for the water, the paint.
        quite aimlessly.
Hush! As though you wanted to
        44. Canvas, paper without
frighten away the scraps and a perfectly
        objective meteor-
ringed apple peel, nibbler.
        dust.
The sunflower seeds spat out care-
        45. Excitement knows no
lessly like mother's idiom. Spit spot
        will, no freedom, no
paint-spot. Carefully figured dots.
        restriction and no desire to
With the softest of pinks comes thought and that opaque
        produce either.
white like pigeon muck. It, you say,
        46. Slowness.

forced itself on me. You draw

47. Neither crowning

a cross into it. The action is

nor beautifying (art).

such that nobody can lose his

48. No hope.

face. The cross, the triangle

49. Does the sun go

done in pencil or otherwise,

down for the sake of beauty?

imprecise. While you suck the seeds.

50. No picture is 'constructed'.

Chew on the aftertaste. Hush. Shade

51. Nothing 'constructed', nothing

in one side of the triangle

'arranged', also nothing

to make the smallest mountainside in the world.

'chaotic'.

Utterly mind's eye. Dart your tongue in

52. Whatever would let itself be arranged?

excitement, form words: scratch,

What could remain chaotic?

scratch, epsilon, aaah, overgrow,

53. A central operator is what's missing.

round round rrrround, too much, where

54. 'Water', 'earth', 'maple',

has it got to. Sentences in the cate-

'oak' are only

gory rhetoric questions, which die

rough divisions.

away in sign-spaces, before you realise

55. River not there to carry

they're there. You control

boats.

what is seen, infallible, nothing escapes you.

56. Mood does not create IT

The lizard's twitching tail in
                    (where should mood
a paler green. As away it
                    come from?), but rather
shoots. Hush. And this disappear-
                    primal excitement, which knows
ing captured on the paper as a scrawly
                    no divisions.
line, right from the start
                    57. Perfect silence through
a variation.
                    perfect fusion.
Thirteen attempts on the fifth of May,
                    58. On the surface of the paper
by late afternoon exhaustion already makes
                    there is no calendar to be found.
itself felt. In the next room, in
                    59. Nothing: indivisible.
the pluperfect, on mother's
                    60. A hole knocked through
divan, mother's cushion, under mother's
                    to the East, a window pushed open
camel-hair blanket, the abandonment to
                    to the light.
sleep, which comes so easily,
                    61. Iwān (place between garden
a pink thought, and nothing to
                    and yard; path) dscham (the being
wash away. Angles, lines, splashes
                    collected of being collected).
carefully kept in their places, the man
                    62. When you sleep you throw the
nowhere.
                    shortest shadow.

60

Steppe

On sight of this happy person

THE BASHKIRIAN ADVENTURE is over. The steppe beckons, this time behind the co-op, where Fräuleins twitch their arms and carve up extra fat salmon. It happens the same way every time: the apples as big as a child's head, no evasion, hooray for ritual until the glass door at the exit opens inwards, rams full bags into your own stomach and sleepily across the street.

But this time the glare, a different green in the sky behind the yellow and white striped awning, from behind the scenes, a gradated green, like sunset at the point where the sun falls behind the hills, night following immediately on its heels, a thing of moments.

The rolling, hilly country of car roofs. Green, the grass is green in the green light of transition —

and there was shown no mercy. Six enormous steppe alsations appeared as though sprung from an ambush and fell with furious barking upon the rider, who spurred his horse —

fell, that the dogs tore him to pieces.

The plains, the hills, the sky and the green distance. The drifting desert thistle. Clumsy, gangling Otto, known as Kasimir, strokes his soft eyebrows. What a happy day today is (brrr)

»a blossoming of strengths and a passionate longing for life«

but further to the left the landscape was unlike yesterday's, Otto Nicolaitch roared with laughter (»grass snakes!«), and the whip cracked down onto some living thing.

Green? Already time to die. Even the grasshopper closed its eyes.

No brightness, no tightness touches me

THE WITHERED STEPPE GRASS, now the sun is locked away. While walking I hear a shrill whistling — screech owl, emergency alarm — the child crashes into the first hurdle only for everything to go wrong *partout*, because the landscape cannot keep you, certainly not alive. The child. I dream it up in the impenetrable blackness. I dream it up as something rustles beside me, the hurdle dreams itself up. To keep fear wide awake.

Where's the sorrel?

Kasimir, be quiet.

O Queen of Heaven, even yesterday that chirping.

Drink your tea.

Far from home, deserted, defenceless and…

Kasimir!

You could misunderstand me...

I can, I could, I am behind all yurts and skyscrapers. In the shopping bag, millet, what was left of it. I can't understand a heaven (holy martyr Barbara) and who is gone to the Moloks? Why is nature on its guard? Neither people nor trees nor shadow. Night surrounds me with an inquisitorial expression. Straight ahead with soundless breath in order to live as a »beautiful, entertaining« woman. I'm so happy I'm sad. I wander about the steppe so as not to tie myself down.

Smile, Kasimir Nicolaitch had said and laid his head in his hands. There!

The gingerbread had gone soft. I chattered away like a magpie.

It does not flicker anymore, the red patch grows smaller and dimmer

THAT'S WHAT THEY call hope. Gaze directed towards the rolling (overcast) horizon because only constancy will work. Please, no flags, no neon signs. Burning anger is good. And sobbing.

From my desk I pace out grassy lowlands and high steppe in turn, surveying. Long forgotten how to kow-tow, the sky is high. O above! Otto Nicolaitch is silent. This time he's silent. He's found bits of bone (white, so white) and can't speak a word. Two tiny red eyes, his.

Otto doesn't fan my fear. Beyond Samara he learned how to handle herds, he knows what binds together. While I'm not yet

63

allowed to lose my mind. The time draws near. Which cloud gives it away? Alright, the grey one with the golden lining, shaped like an otter.

That's what they call hope.

I'm in a confused state of mind. Swing my rod of rosewood — tick, tock — parting hurts. Would arriving be a solution? But where?

»The steppe hid itself in the darkness like Moses Mosevich's children under the blanket.«

The steppe comes and goes. Day in, day out, with a changing wind. With unusual speed, Otto, I chase after the disappearing distance. And behind me: blazing sun and the sustained song.

Write.

Sustained?

Write down the grass.

Anasha, desert candle, Syrian rue, grasshopper, hopper, rip chirping the air, rose-glittering wings. The patch becomes smaller, so small that my staying, his drifting, my staying, his

his

stop.

Otto, I can't see you!

What?

I can only see you dimly.

What?

Through the parting, passed.

What?

You could misunderstand me: I see your absence, Otto, your not-being-there.

What?

Fading pupils.

Write it down!

No calico

AND WITHOUT CAMOUFLAGE into the windy, wild night.
The child plays at robbers. Armed with a piece of glowing
absurdity it stalks about the bushes, the steppe shrubs. I'm a
strong-man! My sensitive son. Your shoulders are no use for a
dispatch rider. He who swings the whip may not despair
(»mama, mama!«) or die of longing. The sky weighs heavy and
much stupidity rolls across the steppe.
Sssssssssh!
I am being quiet.
The nine-year-old hand feels its way through grass that lights
up neon-yellow. Now the beams of light are hopping about like
lolloping rabbits and the child's treble: I've got it! Metal or bits of
bone? Animal or shoe?
In the still light lies the dormouse. So tiny and already dead.
It will need a cross, just like everyone else, says the child, and
puts out the lamp.
Killed.
Why killed?
Ask Kasimir.
I give a slight cough, hopeless.
All the questions, during the night: accident or intention, late
or early, canvas or calico? The child wants to know, now. In the
grainy night.
There are moments when I just don't know what to do next.
And no authority that might. Walking makes it easier. What was
that story about the man whose wife and child were burnt and
who thought his life of little worth and was either silent or talked
of things which had never happened. Either silent or dreaming.
The mouse has a tail and you know —
Nothing at all.
Then the thief threatens attack: Mama, what are you women
good for anyway?

Good for good for ("heaven and earth are full of your glory.")
And above, a star which blinks from beneath the eyelid of
night.

Don't be scared, we're together.

Kasimir

I SUFFERED. And what heightened my suffering were orders:
identity papers for dogs to be presented, singing prohibited, to be
consumed by such and such a date. Dictates of survival, but at
what price. Made to feel small, smaller, smallest, as gnomes we
are controllable. Oh, the sky, Kasimir, I must sing of it. Ever since
I began to step through this life, it has curved up high — a
loneliness, a spell. Not only in Rovnoye, man, — here, where I
don't wear knickerbockers and boots, don't chew on gruel, here
—

cleared his throat. In his hands he held something white,
which at first sight seemed strange, behind his shoulder a shotgun showed. He wasn't drunk, just absent. Give me a glass of tea
and even I would think you a hunter and choir member. By St.
Barbara, you don't bag a bustard for nothing. You drank tea. And
someone laughed loudly and someone sobbed — it was an owl.
I don't know how we started talking. I saw your smoke-coloured
eyes and took courage. You sing? — Now and then. — In church?
— Hardly ever. You didn't ask: why do you ask? Your curved
hand formed a small boat and like a person who has to listen to
heretical discussions, your face closed.

Clumsy clot! someone cried. Your face twitched. Show us the
bustard!

66

Bustard or snipe, to the right the hills shimmered darkly, I was foolish, I followed you into the night.

And then I fell into this state of mind which does without the justification of cause, context, in short, reason. Do you like that, my dear? Not: why do you like that, my dear? Your bass voice is beautiful, you are called Kasimir and Otto, nobody claims that is tautology, nobody claims the ideal is at hand. Sometimes our eyes fall shut in the middle of the day, and we know time is passing. Cautious, the shotgun leans against the sideboard. Check whether snipe are flying over? Oh, the blazing sun and this incessant buzzing of memory — cicadas, hosts of... A big mongrel creeps in. You sit on a ball of wool, the same age as my son, you stare motionless into the distance.

Cross your heart: my favourite look. He leaves nothing out, he strokes your soft eyebrows and moves the horizon. Exit the herd, enter the city traffic. Before a green, before a flaming sky.

In motion?

Yes.

And you will never have arrived.

Yes.

The dog's bark echoes.

When I want to escape him, I wrap myself in felt or calico.

You haven't time for tea and sugar.

Ka-si-mir! I have it and am in it. Only I can't vouch for reality. Is that my steppe? Who will tell me that that's my steppe?

Actually everyone has their own personal steppe. Some never arrive, of course, but all their moves and travels are preparations for the steppe.

Yes. No.

Do you want tea?

Yes. Who will tell me?

Ada, Aidy

1

IN HER HAIR she wears a stiff clip because everything Indian hangs. Control is needed, tamed form. Almond eyes, Aidy would say, discreetly curved nose, a weak squeeze of the hand. Short-sightedness: no comment. The quickest thinker in the city, says Aidy, whoever thinks like that is under the moon's rule, whoever leads his family's fortunes so confidently knows how to capture dreams. Ada, says Aidy, has a pact with world-time. The fine antennae of her hair ends!

Aidy. He asks himself whether he comes from a Trieste or an Agram family. No matter. He is bound to Ada by a passion for the colour yellow and the urge to be on the move.

At the café? Aidy shakes his head. We agreed to go for a walk, and then I will accompany her to the station. What good is sitting, *après tout*.

Walking loosens the last remains of obstinacy and broadens thought. Ada hears the shell-roar of time. She never makes forecasts, for it is offensive to treat time like an object, like that white child's-swing. Along the raked sand-paths, back and forth in fantastic loops. Yellow, the grains of corn which an old woman throws to the pigeons, blue-white-yellow-black the tits that hop quickly across the paths. What is future supposed to be then, a hypothetical present? Aidy says, that doesn't bother me, before and after. Paradisal swimming, agreed?

2

GUSTS OF WIND tear at Ada's sleep. She slips into a dream and starts up in fright, she hears a canary singing and wakes up from the rattling of the blind. Where are you, my moon?

And her body so heavy, as though her legs were pillars. She dreads every November. The November storms dishevel the yellow leaves, whip the rain across the land. Winter is just outside the door. Ada prescribes herself cheerfulness: how brightly the Ganges is flowing, how brightly! And at once rips time asunder with wondrous reading matter and shadow theatres. The lions delight her particularly. From a jungle backdrop Asia roars across to Europe: Indian, Javanese, a blast of trumpets into the heart, she laughs at the blaze of colours. She too is colourful, has painted her eyelids blue.

Night throws you back on yourself. Something in her insists softly, evenly, boundlessly, endlessly: something soft and alluring, something that tempts unceasingly... "Is it happening?" — "No, it's not happening." — "And yet there is something coming." She reads because the regular black lines are comforting. The silent rejection of thought. She reads. Through waiting, that which rejects thought returns to thought. Waiting, space of wandering that does not stray.

The beating of the wind. Not a bird sings, not even at dawn. She waits. Nobody. She reads.

ADA CELEBRATES her thirty-fifth birthday. Aidy comes in with a cake, flown in fresh. Sponge cake, white icing, with five marzipan butterflies on top. *Les papillons pour* Ada! Am I that excited?

> O sister, don't you know the dream
> Of butterfly and linden tree?

Ada kisses Aidy on his beard stubble. You smell of cinnamon, my dear, and have advanced to poet.

The poet scurries across Ada's Bedouin carpet to make some tea. Nursery rhymes! But as far as the transmigration of souls goes... Ada knows the relevant theories. Nothing that isn't cyclical, even Aidy sees himself turning in the wheel of cosmic time, how comforting. As an orphan, he can hope for better things, a sheltered childhood sometime. Complete with pink teddy bears even. New York, though, he wouldn't mind missing out on.

Firstly, metempsychosis, Aidy calls from the kitchen, secondly, love, when Ada interrupts: At six o' clock this evening there's an eclipse of the moon, it will become a blood red disc.

Well timed! Clear night sky.

ADA COMPLAINS. The dreams have become threadbare, "you creep through life Indian-style". Right. The clip still sits firmly in her hair, but waiting uses up waiting energy. Waiting for what? Aidy doesn't ask. Out of the corner of his eyes he tries to catch whether she seems tired, while she focuses her gaze on the Maria-Theresia yellow of the old town-houses as though she were counting the diamonds in a carpet pattern. Determined profile, clear contours, where is hope, thinks Aidy, and has hardly finished his thought when she hisses out: The face is the final, awful frontier.

Like wind howling around the corner of the house.

Then, placatory, are you indisposed?

She suggests a child's treat: a roundabout ride on servile animals! Indian elephant, Shetland pony, Connemara donkey, Canadian husky — ambitious dreams while everything's circling round.

Aidy protests. Not that as well.

As well?

5

NOBODY RELISHES chewing up a disc of lemon as much as Ada. First she turns the pale, sour slice back and forth in her mouth, then she sucks and slurps, not too quietly, no, perfectly audibly and pulls a face. Ada's yellow adventure. *Le repas de la reine*. The lemon wheel is preferred after a small indisposition. Palpitations, the left side of her head aches, fears creep out of every nook and cranny, chewing gives assurance that all is as it should be. Ada chews and Aidy watches.

Watches the unutterably radiant restoration of Ada. He knows the malicious spirits which assault her from time to time. My European night, says Ada, and I dreamed yet again of crowded horse-butchers' shops. Then Aidy fetches the yellow fruit, cuts five slices, lays the largest on her tongue and whispers: Their open mouths meeting in gentle frenzy. Ada is beside herself at the proximity of fulfilment and because the waiting has a certain end.

TODAY, YES, in a middling sort of hotel, yes. Tiny coaches chase across the walls, the carpet is blue as a waterfall.

Most holy…

Sorry?

Most modern.

Eh bien…

The conversation moves in two directions, two bags are in the room.

At sundown of bourgeois comfort…

Aidy smiles.

Ada slips her blouse off and spreads her arms across a mis-coloured cushion. India, India, the youthful dream beyond all barriers, don't let it frighten away the promise of the moment, the bright blue waterfall. When dreams grow into monsters they darken the horizon.

Aidy peels himself out of his gym shoes. The tall mirror promptly reproduces and symmetrically alters every one of his movements.

I hear bleating.

Sorry?

Charming, I hear bleating.

You mean the sheep in that fake Courbet?

Aidy hugs the miscoloured cushion.

Out of pure harmony, sings Ada, and sings no more for Aidy's leopard-skin shirt makes her head spin. Forget Indian heat… Sweat pours down her face and neck. So she continues in a kind of fight with him, in a silent explanation.

NUMBING BRIGHTNESS, like the brightness that glitters over the Aegean, only the Aegean is far away and the season not used to such a flood of light. Every blade of grass shines up individually. Every shadow reinforcing the fact of its existence. Through the curtain of hazel catkins a yellower light makes its way, and where it freezes blue Ada discovers a silent diversity of colour. Under the linden in the park. She doesn't sit down on the grass. She follows the vibration of the light in all its shadings, while the Albanian revolution sounds from a portable radio. Pristina under the linden tree. One way or another, the longer it is the less she knows, because here too knowledge increases ignorance. I drop into Pristina to make sure. She could just as well say, I'm going to take a closer look at the Ganges. And oh, how she searches for solutions. For mother, Fatherland, brother, her own heart through countless sleepless nights! Higher powers — madness. Admittedly, she does like to lose herself in a web of yellow reflections, incommensurable nuances of colour. Aidy finds her lost in contemplation of a tree. She watches, she listens, she is all eye and ear. There goes the tiniest mouse in the world! And if she could have touched the light, she would have kneaded and smoothed, rubbed and caressed it. In idle moments she chases light-hares, which she creates with her pocket mirror.

WORKS OF ART as centres of power, Aidy repeats, Ada doesn't believe a word. She bursts the bulging sentences with a bright laugh. Show-off!

After a little while Aidy asks timidly: What do you see as a non-presumptuous sentence?

Ada: "A little daylight still fell through the words."

Daylight. And now I'm supposed to admit defeat. Ada's lectureship in silence...

AIDY TRIES to punish Ada. Ada tries to win Aidy over to her side. Aidy behaves discreetly, Ada is more colourful than usual. Aidy avoids talk, Ada develops a baroque style of story-telling. Aidy couldn't care less about cinema, Ada goes into raptures over an Indian, an American and an Italian film. Aidy books flights, Ada wants train travel. Aidy gives up wine, Ada allows herself a liqueur. Aidy pleads for speed, Ada praises slowness. Aidy grows pedantic, Ada grows poetic. Aidy says refusal, Ada says desire.

What else?

No return to things outgrown.

No, no, no.

THE EXPULSION from paradise is planned. Or: Despair has long legs. Is anyone in despair?

Au fond, says Aidy, you're breaking my heart. Everyone has cousins and nephews and honey-sweet aunts and siblings and also a past (a personal fable). I only have you.

Yes, says Ada and falls silent.

She debuts her dramatic career with a two-minute scene: fluttering back and forth through the room like a butterfly, to lower herself softly as the colours of the rainbow onto Aidy.

My dear one.

With practised hand, neither young nor damned, she strokes his stubble, humming *Et, sombre, au dessus du Caucase,* somewhere the telephone rings (never mind) and time is suddenly quite new, beyond word and presence.

Aidy doesn't return to his orphan state, Ada doesn't mention her clan. In her hair a majestic butterfly sits resplendent, hovering more beautifully still than her face: and above, Aidy.

So you slip into an afternoon. Shadows fall across the ottoman, Aidy suggests a snack and then a painted Western at the *Nord. Ma reine* Ada.

Yes, Ada is as happy as a princess. She puts the lemon-yellow one on, tailored bodice and full skirt, her butterfly dress. Excited, she fixes another butterfly in her hair — madness of this overflowing afternoon —, calls out to Aidy in a dark, husky voice: To the married couple!

Married couple! echoes Aidy like a model pupil. Better melody than sense.

She shakes her butterfly-bedecked head.

If you forget what I said, then everything's all right.

Very well. Fun or fickleness? Whoever is destined to forget, mutters Aidy, whoever bows to the dictates of forgetting... And suddenly catches sight of the last remains of his solitude, oh, how far distant.

NOTE

Born in 1946, Ilma Rakusa spent her childhood in Budapest, Ljubljana and Trieste before settling in Switzerland where she still lives. She teaches Slavic literature at the University of Zürich and has published a number of anthologies and translations from the Russian, Serbocroatian and French (e.g. Marina Tsvetaeva, Danilo Kis, Marguerite Duras). In 1995, she was Swiss Writer in Residence at the University of Southern California in Los Angeles. Her prizes include the prestigious Petrarca-Prize for translation (1991) and several Ehrengaben of Kanton and City of Zürich.

Steppe (1990) is Rakusa's third book of prose, after a novel (*Die Insel*, 1982), and a volume of stories (*Miramar*, 1986). Since then she has published poems (*Leben. 15 Akronyme*, 1990; *Les mots/morts*, 1992; *Ein Strich durch alles. 90 Neunzeiler*, 1997), "dramolets" (*Jim. 7 Dramolette*, 1993), as well as lectures on poetics (*Farbband und Randfigur*, 1994).

Solveig Emerson, born in 1970 in Cambridge, England, read German at Goldsmiths' College, University of London and took her MA in Literary Translation at the University of East Anglia. She has also translated part of Rakusa's novel, *Die Insel*, and published translations of poems by Ingeborg Bachmann.

Burning Deck Fiction:

Walter Abish, *99: The New Meaning*, 112pp. ISBN 0-930901-67-3 cloth $20; -66-5 paper $8

Tom Ahern, *The Capture of Trieste*, 66pp. ISBN 0-930900-45-6 cloth $15; -46-4 paper $4

Alsion Bundy, *Duncecap*, 128pp.ISBN 1-886224- 23-4 orig. pbk. $10

Barbara Einzig, *Life Moves Outside*, 64pp. ISBN 0-930901-42-8 original paperback $7

John Hawkes, *Innocence in Extremis,* 100pp. ISBN 0-930901-30-4 paper $8

Elizabeth MacKiernan, *Ancestors Maybe*, 160pp. ISBN 0-930901-81-9 original paperback $8

Lissa McLaughlin, *Troubled by His Complexion,* 128pp. ISBN 0-930901-52-5 origial paperback $8
—, *Seeing the Multitudes Delayed,* 76pp. ISBN 0-930900-75-8 cl.$15

Ilma Rakusa, *Steppe,* 80pp. ISBN 1-886224-27-7 originalpbk.$10

Dallas Wiebe, *Going to the Mountain*, 192pp. ISBN 0-930901-49-5 original paperback $10
—, *Skyblue's Essays,* 160pp. ISBN 1-886224-02-1 orig. pbk. $8.95

Please order from Small Press Distribution:
1341 7th St., Berkeley, CA 94710, 1-800-869-7553

New!

Our Asian Journey

~ *A Novel* ~
by
Dallas Wiebe

Thursday, July 3, 1880: I sold my farm today to Praise God Nickel for 875 roubles. When I told my family, Sarah and the children walked around, feeling the bricks of the house, touching the cherry trees, tasting the water from our well. What will they do when I have to sell the cows, the pigs, the furniture? How will I tell Sarah that we cannot take along our wedding clothes? (*from Joseph Toevs' diary, Chapter IV of* **Our Asian Journey**)

In the 1880s a diverse group of Mennonites are compelled by a charismatic leader's enticing words to think that a promised land awaits them in Central Asia, where they believe they will encounter the Second Coming of Christ - while the rest of the world faces the Armageddon. Their leader's tricks of language mingle with

. . . . . (over ☞)

ISBN 0-9692539-9-0
Perfect-bound paper edition; 70 lb (140m) acid-free Finch Vellum Vanilla Opaque paper
450 pages, with coloured end-sheets; 6" x 9" (approx.)
Front-cover colour illustration from a watercolour by Peter Goetz

Only $35.00 (Canadian), $30.00 (U.S.)

Order Form for OUR ASIAN JOURNEY

Name: _____

Address: _____

_____

No. of copies at $35.00 (Canadian), $30.00 (U.S.)/copy (including shipping): _____

Amount of cheque (or money order) enclosed: _____

Please make your cheque or money order payable to:
MLR EDITIONS CANADA

Please mail your order to:
THE EDITOR, MLR EDITIONS CANADA
DEPARTMENT OF ENGLISH
WILFRID LAURIER UNIVERSITY
WATERLOO, ONTARIO N2L 3C5 CANADA

---

this small group of pilgrims' desire for newness in daily life, and so they withdraw their families from the familiar rhythms of Mennonite community life in the Russian countryside and set off on their astonishing trek toward the Orient.

Dallas Wiebe's new novel is a fictionalized account of a series of events that actually took place, mostly in the closing decades of the last century – an account evocative of the hallucinated imagination of some of Wiebe's earlier work. *Our Asian Journey* is a study in the impact of language on individuals and communities. For people governed by a selective, literalistic reading of the Bible and a few other texts, certain words, like the simplest of events, become signs of great significance. For the novel's main character, the gentle and saintly Joseph Toevs, his own words, which he writes down in his diary, finally become his refuge from an otherwise near-surrealistic world. When he is disillusioned not only by the trek to Central Asia, but also by his subsequent emigration to America, words alone – however ambivalently – finally give him hope of a place in a promised land.

~   ~   ~

Dallas Wiebe was born in Newton, Kansas, and grew up there, attending and graduating from Newton public schools. He attended Bethel College in North Newton, Kansas, and graduated with a B.A. in English in 1954. He then studied at the University of Michigan and received his MA in English and American Literature in 1955 and his PhD in English and American Literature in 1960. He taught in universities from 1960 until 1995 when he retired. He lives in Cincinnati, Ohio.

Wiebe's short stories have appeared in *Paris Review, Epoch, North American Review, Black Ice* and elsewhere. In 1978 he won the Aga Khan Fiction Award from *Paris Review* and in 1979 he was published in the Pushcart Awards volume. His novel *Skyblue the Badass* was published in 1969 (Doubleday-Paris Review Editions) and Burning Deck Press has published three volumes of his short stories: *The Transparent Eye-Ball* (1982), *Going to the Mountain* (1988) and *Skyblue's Essays* (1995). Wiebe was a founder and editor of *Cincinnati Poetry Review* through issues 1-24 and is the author of a book of minimalist poems, *The Kansas Poems* (Cincinnati Poetry Review Press, 1987).

~   ~   ~

Our Asian Journey

~ A Novel ~
by
Dallas Wiebe

mr

editions
canada

1997

SIANNE NGAI:
Discredit
Challenging the logic of ownership, credibility and authorial authority, Ngai's poems would risk "losing possession" of themselves in order to raise doubt and disbelief.
Poem, 36 pp., letterpress, 2 colors, ISBN 1-886224-25-0 saddlestitched in wrappers, $8, -26-9 signed, $15

PASCAL QUIGNARD:
Sarx [Série d'Ecriture Supplement #2, trans. Keith Waldrop]
Sarx moves across a landscape of flesh (sarx) and of flesh bitten into (sarcasm). A postmodern *Waste Land*—no King, no Grail, no Question. By the author of Albucius and All the World's Mornings.
Poem, 40 pp., offset ISBN 1-886224-20-x saddlestitched, $5

ILMA RAKUSA:
Steppe [Dichten =, #3, trans. Solveig Emerson]
Love stories? Configurations of encounters, shifting relations, power games, failures. Rakusa explores the tension between the real and the possible, the closeness of love and the claims of the individual. In a language that is both brilliant and simple, cool and intense, spare and eloquent.
Stories, 80 pp., offset, ISBN 1-886224-27-7 original paperback, $10

ALAIN VEINSTEIN:
Even A Child [Série d'Ecriture #11, trans. Robert Kocik and Rosmarie Waldrop]
A poem cannot stop death, even a child's. But here, the very language burrows into the earth, literally, obsessively, in search of the too vulnerable body. Haunting elegies and meditations try to stop time, to encircle the impossible space between not yet and already no more.
Poems, 64 pp., offset, smyth-sewn ISBN 1-886224-28-5 original paperback, $10

KEITH WALDROP
Analogies of Escape
"Will we escape analogy," Claude Royet-Journoud asked. Does Analogies of Escape answer this question? Or does it rather use that famous line as the enigma for a set of variations—a theme always there, under the interplay of verse and prose, but never actually sounded? The author of these "analogies," in any case, finds all analogies, all answers, questionable.
Poems, 80 pp., offset, smythsewn ISBN 1-886224-29-3 original paperback, $10, -30-7 signed, $20

1998 see back /

Winter 1 9 9 8

ALISON BUNDY:
Duncecap
"If a man paints a picture of a beefsteak on a plate very few people will ask, "Who bought that beefsteak? And what did he pay?" The questions are made unnecessary by the rendering of the lush red meat marbled with fat, the light glancing off the white porcelain plate,--I would like the fact of a good sentence to carry similar weight."
"This is rich comic writing, delicate and sure, touched at times by a wistful longing as a kiss might be touched by irony. Or life's violence by the tenderness of dream."—Robert Coover on A Bad Business
Stories, 128pp., offset, smyth-sewn ISBN 1-886224-23-4 original paperback, $10, -24-2 signed, $20

PETER GIZZI:
Artificial Heart
"The most exciting new poet to come along in quite a while" (John Ashbery) here tries to negotiate both artifice and the turbulent domain of feeling -- with an exuberance both familiar and menacing, between embrace and abandonment. Formally a sampling of lyric history from the troubadours to post-industrial punk, it has the haunting quality of a song heard from a distance, overlaid with playground noise, lovers' oaths and cries of loss. The poems both celebrate and challenge the 'spell' of the physical world over the imagination "
Poems, 96 pp. offset, smyth-sewn ISBN 1-886224-21-8 original paperback, $10, -22-6 signed, $20

FORTHCOMING SPRING 1998:

ANNE-MARIE ALBIACH:
A Geometry [Série d'Ecriture Supplement #3, trans. Keith & Rosmarie Waldrop]
Poems, 28 pp., offset, saddlestitched ISBN 1-886224-31-5, $5

XUE DI:
Heart Into Soil: Selected Poems [trans. Keith Waldrop with Wang Ping, Iona Crook, Janet Tan & Hil Anderson]
Poems, ca. 64 pp., offset, smyth-sewn ISBN 1-886224-32-3 original paperback, $10, .

For more information contact:
Rosmarie Waldrop (401) 351-0015

ALISON BUNDY
DunceCap
stories, ca. 128pp., offset, smyth-sewn
ISBN 1-886224-23-4 original paperback, $10
ISBN 1-886224-24-2 original paperback, signed, $20
Publication date: March 15, 1998

> "If a man paints a picture of a beefsteak on a plate very few people will ask, "Who bought that beefsteak? at what shop? And what did he pay?" Those questions are made unnecessary by the skillful rendering of the lush red meat marbled with fat, the light glancing off the white porcelain plate, —I would like the fact of a good sentence to carry similar weight."—Alison Bundy

Alison Bundy was born in 1959 and grew up in Maine. She has an MFA from Brown University and has worked both as a teacher and a plumber. Her prose has appeared in journals like *Ploughshares, Sulfur, Nimrod.* Her first collection of stories, *A Bad Business*, was published by Lost Roads in 1985. *Tale of a Good Cook* was a Paradigm chapbook in 1990.

> Robert Coover said about *A Bad Business:*
> "In these elegant tales—not so much of adventure, comedy, and romance, as of their residue—Alison Bundy summons up the world's distance with a bright paradoxical immediacy that is sometimes almost magical. She is a poet to the prose line born, playing with the possibilities of plot as though it were a metrical system, rhymed with thought's assonantal drift. This is rich comic writing, delicate and sure, touched at times by a wistful loinging as a kiss might be touched by irony. Or life's violence by the tenderness of dream."

Distributors:
Small Press Distribution, 1341 Seventh St., Berkeley, CA 94710
Spectacular Diseases, 83b London Rd., Peterborough, Cambs.PE2 9BS

Burning Deck is pleased to announce
volume 3 of DICHTEN=
(a series of translations of current writing
in German)

For more information contact:
Rosmarie Waldrop (401) 351-0015

ILMA RAKUSA
Steppe
translated from the German by Solveig Emerson
stories, 80 pages, offset, smyth-sewn
ISSN 1077-4203
ISBN 1-886224-27-7, original paperback $10
Publication Date: November 15, 1997

Love stories? Configurations of encounters, shifting relations, power games, failures.
The tension between the closeness of love and the claims of the individual. In a
language that is at the same time brilliant and simple, cool and intense, spare and
eloquent, Rakusa juxtaposes the worlds of the real and the possible.

Born in 1946, Ilma Rakusa spent her childhood in Budapest, Ljubljana and Trieste
before settling in Switzerland. She teaches Slavic literature at the University of
Zürich and has published anthologies and translations from the Russian, Serbocroatian and French. In 1995, she was Swiss Writer in Residence at USC in Los Angeles.
Her prizes include the prestigious Petrarca-Prize for translation (1991).
    Steppe (1990) is her third book of prose, after a novel (*Die Insel*, 1982), and the
stories of *Miramar* (1986).

"Brilliant prose [that] evokes Mallarmé with a throw of dice, and
Proust with states of sleep and memory." — Elke Heinemann, *Die Zeit*

"New perceptions require a new language. [Rakusa] has now achieved
hers: striking, unusual, brilliant."
— Elsbeth Pulver, *Neue Zürcher Zeitung*

"Not theses, but 'voices.' Not unheard-of events, but reflexive writing
that runs to puns. Yet Ilma Rakusa is not interested in mere stylistic
exercises, but in asking a variety of vital questions."
— Hermann Wallmann, *Basler Zeitung*

Solveig Emerson has translated poems by Ingeborg Bachmann. She lives in Hethersett,
England.

Distributors:
Small Press Distribution, 1341 Seventh St., Berkeley, CA 94710
Spectacular Diseases, 83b London Rd., Peterborough, Cambs.PE2 9BS